CHICK 'n' PUG
THE LOVE PUG

For Sweet P.

"My name is Dug. I have just met you, and I love you." —Pixar's *Up*

First published in the United States of America in December 2015
by Bloomsbury Children's Books
www.bloomsbury.com

Bloomsbury is a registered trademark of Bloomsbury Publishing Plc

For information about permission to reproduce selections from this book, write to
Permissions, Bloomsbury Children's Books, 1385 Broadway, New York, New York 10018
Bloomsbury books may be purchased for business or promotional use. For information on bulk purchases
please contact Macmillan Corporate and Premium Sales Department at specialmarkets@macmillan.com

Library of Congress Cataloging-in-Publication Data
Sattler, Jennifer Gordon, author, illustrator.
Chick 'n' Pug : the love pug / by Jennifer Sattler.
pages   cm
Summary: When a new neighbor moves in, Chick can hardly believe his eyes! Daisy is another pug, and she's BEAUTIFUL!
Pug, however, doesn't seem to notice. But Daisy sure notices Pug, and she will do anything to win his affection.
ISBN 978-1-61963-672-9 (hardcover) • ISBN 978-1-61963-673-6 (e-book) • ISBN 978-1-61963-674-3 (e-PDF)
[1. Roosters—Fiction. 2. Pug—Fiction. 3. Dogs—Fiction. 4. Friendship—Fiction. 5. Humorous stories.] I. Title. II. Title: Chick and Pug, the love pug. III. Title: Love pug.
PZ7.S24935Cht 2015   [E]—dc23   2014049128

Art created with acrylics and colored pencil
Typeset in Cafeteria and Draftsman Casual
Book design by Nicole Gastonguay

Printed in China by Leo Paper Products, Heshan, Guangdong
1 3 5 7 9 10 8 6 4 2

All papers used by Bloomsbury Publishing, Inc., are natural, recyclable products made from wood grown in well-managed forests.
The manufacturing processes conform to the environmental regulations of the country of origin.

CHICK 'n' PUG

THE LOVE PUG

Jennifer Sattler

BLOOMSBURY

NEW YORK   LONDON   NEW DELHI   SYDNEY

It was a beautiful day. Chick and Pug
were enjoying some sunshine.

"Oh, she's lovely," said Chick.

"Sure," mumbled Pug. "But so are naps."

"How do you do, Miss Daisy? I'm Chick, and this is my best buddy, Pug. Isn't he magnificent?"

Chick told Daisy about all of
Pug's heroic deeds.
"Oh, my!" She swooned.

Daisy was in love.

She set out to capture the brave and handsome Pug's attention.

And just look at those muscles!

"Well, aren't these pretty?" She sighed.
"I wish *someone* would give me flowers."

"Fear not, dear Daisy!" sang Chick.
"Wonder Pug will get you all the flowers
you need!"

He sure did . . . without even waking up.

But Daisy would never give up that easily.

"Goodness gracious, I've lost my favorite bow!"

"Here it is, Daisy!" said Chick.
"Pug was keeping it safe and warm
for you!"

She had one last idea.

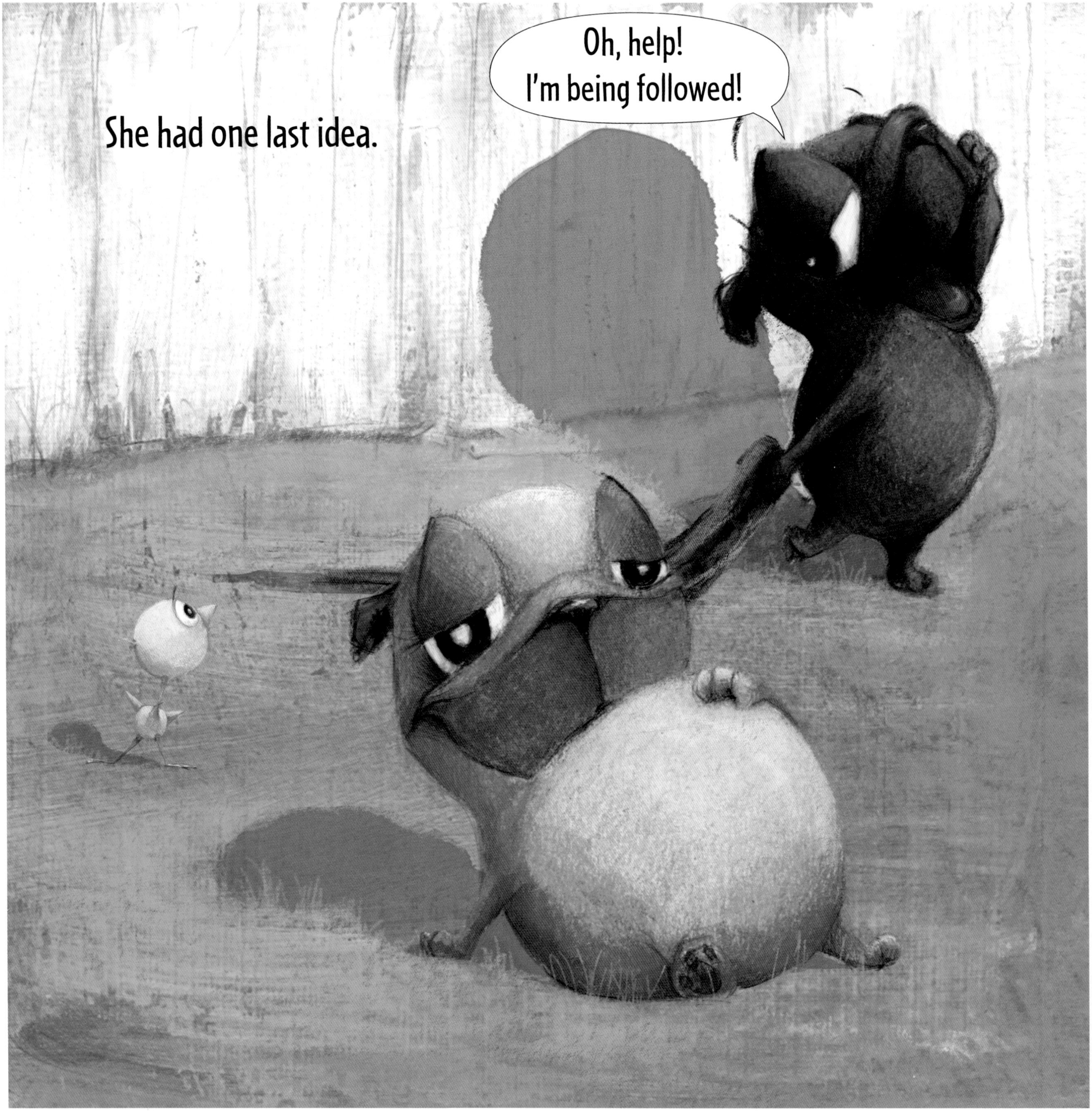

"Nice work, Pug! You scared him away!" Chick was impressed.

Daisy was *not* impressed.

Pug was ready
for another nap.

But suddenly he was *wide* awake!

"Oh, no!" cried Chick.

"Why are Wonder Pug's cheeks buzzing?
Help! Something is terribly wrong!"

"You leave my hero alone, you buzzy rascal!" yelled Daisy.

"Wow." Chick sighed. "What an adventure."

"Yup," mumbled Pug.

Chick and Pug were exhausted.

They weren't the only ones.

After all, sometimes love makes you sleepy.